VULGAR THE VIKING AND THE BATTLE OF BURP

LOOK OUT FOR MORE STORIES OF MAYHEM AND CHAOS IN

VULGAR THE VIKING
AND THE ROCK CAKE RAIDERS

VULGAR THE VIKING
AND THE GREAT GULP GAMES

VULGAR THE VIKING
AND THE SPOOKY SCHOOL TRIP

VULGAR THE VIKING
AND THE TERRIBLE TALENT SHOW

VULGAR THE VIKING
AND A MIDSUMMER NIGHT'S SCREAM

Vulgar the Viking and the Battle of Burp

ODIN REDBEARD

ILLUSTRATED BY
SARAH HORNE

nosy
crow

With special thanks to
Barry Hutchison

First published in the UK in 2013 by Nosy Crow Ltd
The Crow's Nest, 10a Lant St
London, SE1 1QR, UK

Nosy Crow and associated logos are trademarks and/or
registered trademarks of Nosy Crow Ltd

Text copyright © Hothouse Fiction, 2013
Illustrations © Sarah Horne, 2013

The right of Hothouse Fiction and Sarah Horne to be identified as the author
and illustrator respectively of this work has been asserted by them in accordance
with the Copyright, Designs and Patents Act 1988.

Printed and bound in the UK by Clays Ltd, St Ives Plc

Papers used by Nosy Crow are made from wood grown in sustainable forests.

ISBN: 978 0 85763 218 0

www.nosycrow.com

CHAPTER ONE

HISTORY LESSONS

Vulgar sat near the back of the class, drumming his dirty fingernails on the school desk. His teacher was droning on about an old battle. A battle should have been an exciting subject for a lesson, but the teacher wasn't called Dagmar the Dull for nothing.

"It took the Viking forces a great many hours to row their longboats to Angle

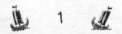

Land," said Dagmar. "During this time they encountered all manner of dangers and perils."

"Like sea serpents?" Vulgar asked hopefully.

"Like hand splinters," Dagmar said. "And possibly even some light rain."

Vulgar's shoulders slumped. "Oh."

He looked over to his best friend Knut's desk. Knut's wonky horned helmet was down over his eyes and he was snoring gently.

"What about the battle itself?" asked Vulgar. "Can we skip to that bit?"

"Hour after hour they rowed," droned Dagmar, ignoring him. "With only the waves for company."

"And two hundred other Vikings," pointed out Princess Freya. She was sitting at the front of the class, her long blonde hair tied in perfect pigtails. Luckily for her, Vulgar couldn't quite reach them from his seat.

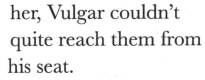

Dagmar ignored her, too. "When they finally reached the village of Burp they were exhausted and slightly damp, but they were ready to fight. They had a tall task ahead of them. A very tall task, indeed.

For they needed to capture the famous Burp Tower, in order to pillage its stores of gold!"

"Now we're talking," said Vulgar. He jabbed a pinkie finger in his ear and wiggled out a lump of wax. He wanted to hear every word of this.

Even Knut had opened his eyes and was listening intently. "I bet we destroyed them," Vulgar said. "How long did it take?"

"About half an hour, I bet," guessed Knut.

"Less," said Vulgar. "We conquered

them and got the gold in about ten minutes. Right?"

Dagmar shook his head. "Wrong. The Viking invaders were driven back by the people of Burp."

Vulgar's jaw dropped. He flicked out another clump of wax, in case he'd misheard. "Driven back?"

"Defeated. Vanquished. Sent packing," Dagmar said.

Vulgar and Knut exchanged disbelieving glances. "But... but how?"

"It's actually very interesting," said Dagmar, and Vulgar immediately knew it wouldn't be. "They employed a technique we refer to as the 'Boar's Snout'."

"What? They were riding on pigs?" said Knut.

"The 'Boar's Snout' is a battle formation," explained Dagmar. "Soldiers form into an arrowhead shape. This pushes through the opposing army, scattering them. The people of Burp drove back the invading Vikings, and stopped them from stealing any gold."

"So… what?" muttered Vulgar, who was still coming to terms with the fact that the Vikings had lost. "We got beaten by a big triangle?"

"Still, a triangle with a cool name," said Knut. "Boar's snout." He snorted like a pig. Vulgar laughed, then snorted noisily back in reply.

Freya turned and glared at them. "Cut it out. That's disgusting."

"I thought you'd like it, being a pig yourself," Vulgar replied. He snorted again, even louder this time.

"Yes, I *am* a PIG," Freya said, folding her arms. "A Pretty Intelligent Girl."

"Yeah, well..." said Vulgar, but he couldn't think of a reply, so he just gave a final piggy snort instead.

The teacher carried on talking about the Battle of Burp, but Vulgar had lost interest. He sat back in his chair and gazed out of the window instead.

The people of Blubber were going about their usual business. They tended their vegetables. They trimmed their grass. They crochctcd and knittcd.

None of it was proper Viking stuff.

If they'd won the Battle of Burp things might have been different. If they'd won back then, maybe school wouldn't have been invented. *I'd be out pillaging and plundering now, not sitting in a boring old classroom*, thought Vulgar.

A blast of a horn snapped him out of his daydream. The fanfare continued for a few seconds, then collapsed into a fit of coughing and wheezing. An old man hobbled into the class, struggling to get his breath back. It was Harrumf, the steward of the Great Hall. "Nearly blew me bleedin' lungs out," Harrumf muttered, before he realised the whole class was looking

8

at him. "Show yer appreciation for His
Royalness—" Harrumf began, before
another coughing fit made him stop.

King Olaf waddled into the class
munching on a barbecued elk rib. Gravy
dripped down his chin and into his plaited
beard.

"Greetings, children,"
he said, spraying little
lumps of elk meat
over the front row.

"Good morning,
King Olaf," the
class chorused,
ducking to avoid
the worst of
the spray.

"As Dagmar has no doubt told you, this week sees the one hundredth anniversary of the Battle of Burp."

"Actually," said Dagmar, raising a crooked finger, "historians are unable to reach an agreement on the exact date of—"

"Blah, blah, blah," said King Olaf, waving a dismissive hand. "To celebrate, I'm taking you all on a trip to Angle Land, where we will be re-enacting the battle itself."

"Hooray!" cheered the class.

"I can't go. I get seasick," said Dagmar.

"You weren't invited," said the King.

"Hooray!" cheered the class, even louder this time.

Vulgar raised a hand. "Angle Land is across the sea. How will we get there?"

Please say longboat, please say longboat, please say longboat, he thought.

"By longboat," said King Olaf, and
Vulgar jumped off his seat in excitement.
He and Knut began dancing around the
classroom.

"We're going on a longboat!" Knut
shouted.

"To invade Angle Land!" added Vulgar.

King Olaf raised his hands. "Whoa there! Nobody said anything about *invading*."

Vulgar and Knut stopped dancing.

"We're going to celebrate one hundred years of friendship between Blubber and Burp," the King explained. "This is a trip to promote peace and harmony."

Vulgar thought about this. "But we're still going by longboat?"

"Yes," said King Olaf. "We're still going by longboat."

Vulgar shrugged and started dancing again. He was going to sail the seas on a real longboat, just like a proper Viking. This was going to be brilliant!

CHAPTER TWO

LONGBOATS ARE NOT BRILLIANT

Vulgar's mum, Helga, peered suspiciously into his knapsack. The bag looked tiny in her enormous, shovel-like hands.

"Why is your bag full of elk manure?" she asked.

Vulgar looked at his reflection in the water basin. Still no beard. He'd hoped one might have sprouted overnight, ready for his longboat adventure.

"For juggling with," replied Vulgar, as if that explained everything.

Helga shook her head. "No. You're not taking elk manure," she said, shoving her hand into the bag. Along with the manure, she pulled out a slimy green ball.

"No fair," whined Vulgar. "I can't take my bogey collection?"

With a shudder, Helga tossed the contents of the knapsack across the room. Vulgar's dad, Harald, chose

that moment to enter the kitchen. He let out a sharp scream and ducked his scrawny body just in time. The manure and bogey mixture made a loud, gloopy *shplatt* as it landed in the waste bin.

Helga began cramming other things into the knapsack. "You'll need a jumper, in case it gets cold. Some reindeer jerky, in case you get hungry. A comb."

"In case my hair gets messy?"

"Your hair is *always* messy, Vulgar."

15

Vulgar tried to smooth down the tufts of hair sticking out beneath his helmet. They immediately *boinged* back up again.

"Have you given him clean pants?" asked Harald.

"I'm only going for two nights!" Vulgar protested. "I don't need clean pants."

"Yes, you do," Helga said, shoving a pair of itchy grey underpants into the bag. She spat on her thumb and wiped a smudge off Vulgar's face.

"Ew, get off!" Vulgar yelped.

"Stay still," Helga barked. She said it so sharply that both Vulgar and Harald froze. "You'd

better mind your manners when you're in Angle Land. They're very proper over there, so be on your best behaviour."

Then Helga hugged Vulgar so hard his eyes began to bulge. "I'm going to miss you," she sniffled.

"Can't… breathe…" gasped Vulgar. His mum let him go and he took a big breath.

"Here, take these," said Harald, passing him a bag of rock cakes. "But they're not for you. They're for the family you're staying with."

"It's a bravery medal they need, not cakes," Helga muttered.

Vulgar took the bag and peered in at the cakes. He hoped the brown flecks on the outside were burnt bits. You had to check brown bits very carefully when your dad cleaned toilets for a living.

Grunt, Vulgar's scruffy dog, snored gently beneath the kitchen table. Vulgar rubbed his head. "See you, boy," he said.

HONK! Grunt jumped awake and bolted out of the room in fright as Helga noisily blew her nose. Vulgar decided to run before the hugging started again.

"See you soon," he said, rushing for the door.

"Be good," Harald said. "And don't eat the rock cakes."

"As if I would," called Vulgar, and he darted off down the path.

"Take care, my little walrus whisker!"

sobbed Helga. Vulgar waved, slipped his knapsack on to his back, then set off in the direction of the harbour.

It was six o'clock in the morning. Vulgar was surprised so many people were already up and about, tending to their gardens and doing chores. They all waved to him as he raced through the village.

"Cheerio, Vulgar!"

"Happy crossings!"

"Get off my flower bed!"

He almost ran straight into Knut, who was slouching sleepily towards the harbour, his helmet tilted so far to one side Vulgar couldn't understand how it was staying on.

"All right?" Knut said.

"All right? I'm *brilliant*!" shouted Vulgar. "We're going on a longboat!"

They did their longboat dance again, then carried on.

"I bet it looks terrifying," Vulgar said. "To other people, I mean. Not Vikings. We're not scared of anything."

"Except trolls," said Knut.

"Well, yeah..."

"And vegetables."

"Right..."

"And—"

"We're not scared of longboats, though," Vulgar said.

"I bet it'll be carved into

the shape of a big dragon or something!"

They reached the docks and there it was, sitting low in the water straight ahead – the longboat. They started to cheer until they spotted the figurehead at the front. It wasn't in the shape of a dragon, or a troll, or even an unusually large vegetable.

The figurehead had been carved into the shape of a girl with long plaits. It looked almost exactly like Princess Freya.

"Yuck," Vulgar groaned. "What a waste of wood."

He yelped as a fist thumped his arm. "I heard that," snapped Freya. "My dad had that carved specially in my honour," she explained.

"To scare off sea serpents, probably," Vulgar muttered.

The princess skipped off towards the boat. The other children from school were already gathering around the gangplank that led on to the deck. Harrumf was standing beside them, waving his stick and barking orders.

"Right, all aboard. Two at a time. Stop pushing!"

Vulgar and Knut ducked past him and scurried along the gangplank. The deck was long and thin, with rows of benches on either side. Vulgar slid on to a bench near the back, with Knut sitting

behind him. The bench didn't feel very
comfortable. Vulgar would've asked for
a cushion, but he thought proper
Vikings probably didn't bother
with cushions.

When the children had all taken their
seats, King Olaf shuffled down the
gangplank.

As he heaved himself on to the deck
the boat tipped dangerously to one side.
Children screamed and clung to
their benches to stop themselves
sliding overboard.

The king moved to the middle of the
deck and the boat settled back
into an upright position. "Right
then," he said, clapping his hands

together. "Are we ready for the off?"

Vulgar pointed up to the ship's mast. It rose up like a tree trunk from the deck. "We haven't put the sail up," he said.

"There's no wind," said Harrumf.

"Then how are we supposed to get there?"

Harrumf pointed a crooked finger at a pole that poked through a hole in the side of the boat beside Vulgar.

"Them's oars," said Harrumf. "You want to get to Burp? You'd best get rowin'!"

With a groan, Vulgar took hold of the oar. All across the deck, the other children did the same. "All together now," urged Harrumf. "'Eave! 'Eave! Come on, put yer backs into it!"

Vulgar and the others dragged the oars through the water. They heaved and strained against the tide, pulling with all their might for what felt like hours. On and on they went until Vulgar's arms burned with the effort.

"How far have we gone?" he panted. Surely they were almost there by now?

King Olaf cupped his hands around his eyes to shield them from the sun. He stared back the way they'd come. "About six metres," he said.

Vulgar *thonked* his head against the side of the boat. This was going to be a very long trip.

Hours later, when the harbour was finally out of sight and the ocean surrounded them on all sides, Vulgar stopped rowing. His whole body ached but, more importantly, he was bored. He and Knut had already eaten all the reindeer jerky, and they'd wolfed down the rock cakes in a matter of seconds.

Vulgar looked across the deck. Princess Freya was sitting just a few rows ahead of him, rowing hard.

"Watch this," he whispered to Knut, then he crept up behind the princess. "Sea-serpent attack!" he cried, leaping on to Freya's back.

With a yelp, Freya caught hold of Vulgar's arm and flipped him over her shoulder. For a moment, Vulgar felt himself hanging in mid air, and

then he plunged over the side of the
ship and splashed into the freezing water
below.

"Oh dear," sang a voice from up on
deck. Treading water, Vulgar looked up to
see Freya smiling down at him. "Silly me,
I thought you were a sea serpent."

"G-get m-me out," Vulgar stammered.

"Of course I will," said Freya. "Once
you say sorry."

"Wh-what?"

"Unless you don't *need* my help..."

"S-sorry," Vulgar yelped. The cold water
was turning his skin blue, and he was sure
he'd just felt a real sea serpent brush past
his feet. "S-sorry! Now g-get m-me out!"

With a triumphant grin, Freya tilted her
oar so Vulgar could climb up it. Shivering,
he squelched back on to his seat and took
hold of the oar. This trip was turning out
to be terrible.

"S-still," he mumbled. "At least it c-can't get any worse."

BLEEEURGH!

Something warm and smelly splattered against the Vulgar's back. He turned to see a green-looking Knut wiping the corners of his mouth.

"Sorry, Vulgar," Knut groaned. "I get seasick."

"On second thoughts," Vulgar sighed, "maybe it can get worse."

CHAPTER THREE

IT GETS WORSE

"Eyes to starboard, there's a big blue whale,
Eyes to port, see the mermaid's tail,
Out in the water, hear the oars go splash,
Down in the galley there be jerky and mash."

Vulgar groaned. Not another sea shanty!
King Olaf had been singing for hours,
although it felt like days. Thinking about
it, Vulgar couldn't remember a time

when King Olaf *hadn't* been singing a sea shanty.

The singing was bad enough, but his dancing was the real problem. Every time the King jigged across the deck, the boat tossed around in the water like a toy in a bathtub.

It was becoming clear to Vulgar why the people of Blubber had given up their sea-faring ways. The sea was rubbish. He never thought he'd say this, but longboats were rubbish, too. His hands were blistered from the oars, and the hard wooden seat meant he hadn't been able to feel his bum in hours. His bottom was so numb it could catch on fire and he wouldn't know it until he smelled the smoke.

The excited chatter that had filled the deck for the first half hour or so had quickly turned to grumbling. Now there

was no sound on the ship other than
the creaking of oars and King Olaf's
warbling.

"Here's one for you," King Olaf
boomed. "It's an old favourite of mine
called 'Three Hundred Reasons Why the
Sea is Wet'."

Just then a
cry came from
the crow's
nest up
above them.

"Land-ho!" called Harrumf. "Burp dead ahead."

A gasp went up all across the deck. The children craned their necks to get their first glimpse of Angle Land.

Dark rain clouds dotted the grey sky. Through a curtain of drizzle Vulgar could just make out some cliffs with a tower perched on top. *That must be where all the gold is*, thought Vulgar. He and the other children began to pull harder on the oars, and soon the longboat floated into the Burp harbour.

"Oi, quit pushin', you lot," shouted Harrumf from the top of the mast, as all the children raced to get off the boat. "Wait there. One at a time. 'Is Royalness first!"

No one paid him any attention.

Vulgar, Knut and the other children hobbled up the gangplank and took their first shaky steps on Angle Land.

"Just you wait," Harrumf bellowed. "Yer all in big trouble now. I'm coming down, and then yer all for the... 'Ere, who's nicked me ladder?"

A crowd of villagers had gathered on the docks. Vulgar had been picturing what they would look like, these people who had fought off a Viking invasion. He was expecting hardened warriors with yellow teeth, bulging muscles and beards big enough to live in. And the men would be even worse.

Instead, the villagers looked much like those back in Blubber. Most of them were quite scrawny, and they were all disappointingly clean-shaven. He was right about the teeth, though.

"Top-ho, what?" boomed an imposing woman at the front of the group. She had a long face that reminded Vulgar of a horse. Her light-brown hair was scraped back in a bun, and she wore green boots that were caked with mud. "Jolly good rowing, chaps. Jolly good indeed."

"I'm not stuck up 'ere, you know? I can climb like a goat, me," called Harrumf, but everyone continued to ignore him.

"Ah, Lady Edith," boomed King Olaf. "What an honour it is to meet you at last," he said, bowing low.

"Nonsense!" cried Lady Edith, curtsying slightly. "The honour is all mine, your majesty. It is with great delight that I welcome you to our humble land."

"And it is with equal, if not much greater delight, that we arrive here in our modest ship," King Olaf countered, his voice even louder. Vulgar noticed

that every time Lady Edith or King Olaf
spoke, they puffed their chests further out.

"Truly our harbour is not fit to play host
to such a handsome vessel," said Lady
Edith, her voice growing louder with
every word.

"No, my lady, it is *our* ship that does your harbour an injustice," King Olaf said, raising his voice so it was even louder still. "I've a good mind to burn the wretched thing, rather than have it sully this fair land of yours."

"Delightful of you to say so, your majesty, but I must—"

"Aaaargh!"

THUD!

All eyes turned to the ship. Harrumf lay on the deck in a tangled heap.

"I meant to do that," he insisted, but the way his legs were wrapped around his neck made Vulgar suspect he hadn't.

"Oh dear, has your monkey been injured?" asked Lady Edith.

King Olaf blinked. "Monkey? That's not a monkey, that's my steward."

Lady Edith peered long and hard at Harrumf. "I say," she muttered at last, then she shook her head. "Well, let's not beat around the bush any longer, what? It's time for the children to meet their host families." She clapped her hands sharply and everyone, including King Olaf, jumped. "Come along, children," she barked, then she turned and strode towards the gathered villagers.

The children were introduced to the families they would be staying with. Knut was to be looked after by a little old lady who kept pinching his cheek and laughing at his helmet. The helmet hadn't looked right since he'd snapped off one of the horns and accidentally stuck it back on upside down.

"He's a bag of bones, this one," the old woman said, giving Knut's cheek another squeeze. "You needs fattening up. I'll feed you till you burst!"

"Help," Knut whispered, but Vulgar was busy being introduced

to his own host family.

"I'm Bert," said a cheerful-looking man with a red face. The smell of fish hung around him like a cloud. "This is Bertha," he continued, introducing his wife. She was just as cheerful-looking, but not quite as red in the face. Looking around at some of the other host families, Vulgar thought he could've done a lot worse.

"Come on," said Bertha with a smile. "Let's get you home."

Bert and Bertha's hut was even more fishy-smelling than Bert himself. Bert was a fisherman. The odour was so strong that Vulgar wondered if Bert brought the fish home to live with them after he'd caught them.

As Vulgar stepped through the door, something red and squidgy splattered against his helmet and dripped down into his hair.

"Bullseye!" cried a high-pitched voice.

"What a shot!" yelped another.

Vulgar looked up to see two boys hanging from a fishing net on the ceiling. They had tightly curled red hair and freckles dotted all over their faces. For a moment, Vulgar thought he was seeing double.

"The twins," Bert explained. He wiped a clump

of tomato off Vulgar's shoulder. "Sorry about that."

"Albert, Gilbert, cut that out," warned Bertha.

The twins giggled, then clambered down from the ceiling.

"Fancy a cuppa?" asked Bert. He pushed a cup of something grey and steaming under Vulgar's nose. It smelled like his mum's feet.

"No, thanks."

"What's it like where you live?" asked Albert.

"Is it really boring being a Viking?" asked Gilbert.

Vulgar puffed out his chest. "No," he said. "It's not boring. It's really exciting.

We, um, fight trolls all day. And I go to school on a reindeer."

The twins looked almost impressed by this. "You've got a reindeer?"

"Yes," said Vulgar. "And a pet dragon." He bit his lip. He'd gone too far. They'd never believe that one.

"A *dragon*!" gasped the twins. Their eyes went wide at exactly the same time. "That's amazing!"

"Nothing exciting ever happens in Burp," sighed Albert. "All they ever do is go fishing."

"Raaaaar!" roared Gilbert. "I'm a dragon," he said, then he kicked Vulgar up the bum.

"No kicking, Gilbert," warned his mum.

"Aw, but I was being a dragon," Gilbert muttered.

"Dragons don't kick," said Bert. "They set things on fire."

Bertha gave her husband a long, hard look.

"Actually, they don't do that either," Bert said quickly. "They tidy their rooms and eat all their dinner. That's what dragons do."

The twins bombarded Vulgar with questions until dinner was ready. Vulgar told them all about Viking school, where you learn how to wrestle giants and tame polar bears. The boys believed every word.

Vulgar's stomach rumbled as they sat down to eat. Something squidgy was plonked on to his plate. He gave it a prod as the family began to eat.

"Tuck in.'S nice," said Gilbert.

"I'll have it if you don't want it," Albert said.

Vulgar remembered what his mum had said about being polite. He picked up the squidgy thing and took a very small bite. It *boinged* like rubber, then squelched a horrible salty flavour in his mouth. It was the foulest thing he had ever tasted in his life.

"It's sea snail," said Albert with a grin, and Vulgar instinctively spat the mouthful across the room. It bounced off the wall and fell to the floor.

"Sorry," he said quickly. "I'm, um, allergic to sea snail."

"Not to worry," said Bert. He held out a little pot filled with what looked like slime. A single fishy eye peered up out of the sludge. "Jellied eel?"

"Or there's black pudding," said Bertha.

"Made from pig's blood," added Gilbert.

Vulgar stood up. "Actually," he said, yawning, "I'm really tired. Is it OK if I head to bed?"

"Of course," said Bert. "Boys, show Vulgar where the bed is."

The twins led Vulgar to the big straw bed they were going to be sharing. He kicked off his boots and slipped under the rough blanket. His body was aching from the rowing. A good night's sleep was just what he...

AARGGHH! Something cold and wet touched his bare feet. Vulgar yelped with fright and leapt out of the bed. Albert and Gilbert fell about laughing as they pulled back the blanket to reveal a slimy dead fish.

"Gotcha!" Albert giggled.

"I guess you don't learn the 'fish in a bed' trick at Viking school," chortled Gilbert.

Vulgar picked the stinky fish up and went to toss it out of the window.

"Hey! Don't throw that out," cried Gilbert. "That's tomorrow's breakfast!"

Laughing, the twins skipped off again, leaving Vulgar to climb back into the fishy-smelling bed. In less than a minute, he was fast asleep.

CHAPTER FOUR

THE GRAND TOUR

Vulgar awoke to find a toe up his nose
and an elbow digging into his back.
He thought maybe his dog, Grunt,
had jumped on to the bed, but then
remembered he was in Angle Land.

He removed Albert's toe from his nostril,
nudged Gilbert's elbow away from his
back, then clambered out of the bed. He
moved quietly so he didn't wake the twins.

He wasn't sure he could handle them so
early in the morning.

He silently slipped a foot into one of
his boots, then he cried out in shock as
something prickly jabbed
at his toes. Albert
and Gilbert
immediately
erupted in
laughter.
Vulgar turned
his boot
upside-down
and a starfish
plopped on to
the floor.

"Very funny,"
he sighed, tipping
a half-chewed sea snail out of the other
boot. He shoved his feet inside and
stomped off in search of breakfast.

Breakfast turned out to be the fish, just as the twins had promised, so he gave it a miss. Instead, he headed off to the village green to meet the other children from his class.

"Hey, wait up!" called Albert, running after him.

"We're coming too!" shouted Gilbert, following behind.

Knut was already there, his cheeks red from being constantly pinched by the old woman. Harrumf was there as well, limping even more than usual after his fall from the crow's nest. The only Blubberers Vulgar couldn't see were Princess Freya and King Olaf. He eventually spotted them marching down the hill with Lady Edith. King Olaf and Lady Edith were powering ahead, each trying to walk faster than the other. Freya hurried along behind, doing her best to keep up.

"Morning all, morning
all," brayed Lady Edith as she
approached the group.

"Morning all," added King Olaf, in a
slightly louder voice.

"Here," whispered Gilbert, suddenly
appearing at Vulgar's side. "Why aren't

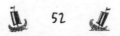

you showing your pants?"

Vulgar blinked. "Er… what?"

"Showing your pants," said Albert, appearing on the other side. "In Angle Land, visitors are supposed to show their pants to important people."

"It's tradition," added Gilbert.

"It's rude not to show your pants," said Albert.

"Hurry!" whispered Gilbert. "Or you'll get in trouble!"

"Show her your pants or she'll chuck you in the dungeon!" There was no time to lose. As Lady Edith and King Olaf reached the gathered crowd, Vulgar whipped down his shorts, revealing his dirty grey pants beneath.

"Wiggle your bum, quick!" Gilbert
urged.

Vulgar wiggled like he'd never wiggled
before. Lady Edith stopped dead in her
tracks. Her eyes went wide. Her mouth
fell open. A shriek of outrage pierced the
drizzly morning air.

"How *dare* you?" she demanded. Albert
and Gilbert turned away to hide their
laughter, and Vulgar quickly pulled up
his shorts. He had to admit that it was a
pretty good trick – if only he'd thought of
it himself he could have used it on Freya.
He just hoped he wasn't about to be
thrown in the dungeon.

"Sorry," he said quickly.

"One does *not* waggle one's buttocks at
a lady!" Lady Edith roared.

"We do where we come from," said
Princess Freya, slightly out of breath from
trying to keep up. "In Blubber, showing

someone your pants is a sign of great respect."

Lady Edith frowned. "Is it?"

King Olaf glared at Vulgar, but did his best to cover for him. "Oh yes. Definitely. Want to show someone you respect them? Show them your pants, that's what we always say." He turned around. "Here, let me show you mine."

"Please don't!" barked Lady Edith. She clapped her hands, and once again everyone jumped. "Come along. Let us begin the tour. There is much to see."

She marched off, leaving King Olaf racing to catch up. The children filed off after them, but Vulgar pulled Freya aside.

"Um, thanks," he said.

"Don't mention it," said Freya. "She deserved it. She had us up all last night bragging about how great Angle Land is." The princess smiled sweetly. "Besides, now you owe me one."

She skipped off to join the rest of the group. Vulgar tagged along behind, followed by the giggling twins. Today was *not* off to a good start.

The tour didn't help. Lady Edith took them to a large statue commemorating the Battle of Burp. It showed a ferocious Viking warrior being hit on the head by an old woman with a frying pan. If you looked really closely, you could see the Viking was crying.

After that, they'd been introduced to Burp's favourite pastime – cheese rolling, which was just as boring as it sounded.

Next they had been "treated" to some traditional music from Angle Land. A man had appeared carrying what looked like an octopus under one arm. He blew into a pipe attached to it and the octopus inflated. A terrible drone emerged from

The Battle of Burp

somewhere within it.

"Bagpipes," explained Lady Edith. She tapped her foot in time with the music.

"It sounds like a troll choking on a goat," Vulgar said, but no one was able to hear him.

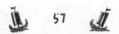

Finally, it was time for the highlight of the tour, the moment Vulgar had been waiting for.

"Behold!" cried Lady Edith, in her loudest, grandest voice. "The site of the Battle of Burp!"

This was it! Vulgar held his breath. He'd never seen a real battlefield before. There would be swords and skulls and body parts

lying around, he was sure. This was going to be brilliant.

Lady Edith stepped aside to reveal… a field. It was completely empty, aside from four bored-looking sheep munching grass near the far end.

"Where are the weapons?" Vulgar groaned. "Where's the blood?"

"It's been a hundred years," Freya told him. "They've tidied up."

"Onwards, children," clucked Lady Edith, leading them towards the cliffs.

They puffed and panted all the way to the top, where the stone tower stood looking out to sea. Jutting out from the tower was a flag pole, flying the Angle Land flag.

"The tower, of course, was built two hundred years ago to protect Burp and house our gold. Impressive, what?" she said.

King Olaf shrugged. "Not bad."

"Not bad?" Lady Edith spluttered. "Why, its walls are almost a metre thick."

"*Almost* a metre?" asked the King. "The walls of my castle are *exactly* a metre thick."

"Well these ones were jolly well strong enough to keep you Vikings out and stop you capturing the Burp gold, what?" Lady Edith snorted.

King Olaf smiled politely. "Only because we weren't really trying."

"That's the problem with you foreign chaps. Afraid of a little hard work."

King Olaf opened his mouth to reply, but Lady Edith was already marching back down the hill.

"Come along. It's time to make weapons for the battle re-enactment."

Vulgar looked at Knut and they both grinned. Weapon making – now *that* sounded like fun!

The children were each given wood, tools and paints and left to get on with it. Vulgar painted some red blood on his wooden sword, then set to work decorating his shield.

The Burp children didn't need to make weapons, but Gilbert and Albert had been following Vulgar around all day. It was like having two miniature shadows. Only these shadows never stopped talking and getting in the way.

"Ooh, scary," said Albert, watching Vulgar paint a fire-breathing dragon.

"Not really," said Vulgar, adding a dab of red paint. "Or at least *I* don't find dragons scary. Once you've tamed a few of them, you don't think anything of it."

The twins stared at him, their eyes round.

"You should've painted a fish," Gilbert suggested. "The way you screamed last night, you must think fish are *really* terrifying."

"Stand up so we can see it properly," Albert urged. Vulgar hesitated, then stood and held up the sword and shield for the brothers to see.

"You know, it *is* pretty cool," Albert admitted.

"Yeah, good work, Vulgar," said Gilbert.

Vulgar smiled. "Thanks," he said, then he sat down.

PAAARP! A loud trumping noise came from Vulgar's bottom.

Freya stared at him. "That was *disgusting!*" she gasped.

Albert and Gilbert fell about laughing. Vulgar reached down and pulled something out from under him.

"Inflated pig's bladder," Albert giggled.

"Oldest trick in the book!" Gilbert laughed.

Vulgar shook his head. He couldn't believe the twins had got him again. It was time to show the Terrible Two who was boss. If they wanted trumping noises, he'd give them trumping noises!

Vulgar tucked his hand under his armpit, and made the loudest, trumpiest noises ever heard in Burp.

PAAARP! PAAAAARRPP! PAAAAAAAAAARP!

The twins clapped with delight. "More!" they called.

Using his other armpit, Vulgar gave them more – a series of explosive *PAAAAARPS!* to the tune of "Ingrid Had a Little Elk".

Gilbert cheered.

"That was AMAZING!" cried Albert.

"*That's* how Vikings do it," said Vulgar.

The twins ran off, trying to make trump noises with their armpits.

Vulgar checked his seat, then sat back down to finish decorating his shield. How was it possible that Blubber had lost to these people? They didn't even know how to make proper fart noises! And that tower that Lady Edith kept bragging about didn't look any harder to break into than his mother's biscuit tin – and he'd managed that before.

He suddenly had a thought. The people of Burp may have won the battle the first time around, but that didn't mean the Vikings couldn't learn from their mistakes.

The next day wouldn't be a repeat of the Battle of Burp. It would be the Battle of Burp... round two!

CHAPTER FIVE

THE BATTLE OF BURP II

The children of Blubber and Burp stood on the battlefield, the morning mist swirling around them. In keeping with tradition, the Burp children were armed with pots, pans and other kitchen utensils.

Vulgar had spent the evening before telling the twins stories about all the battles he'd won in the past. He may have exaggerated a teeny, tiny bit, but the twins

didn't seem to notice. They couldn't get enough of his stories.

"Tell us about the time you raided a dragon's cave and stole all his treasure," begged Gilbert.

"And the time you fought off a whole army of trolls one-handed," said Albert eagerly.

"Maybe later," said Vulgar. He went over to talk to his friends.

Freya's sword was pink with yellow flowers on it, and she had painted a heart on her shield. She looked sweet, but Vulgar knew that she was anything but.

"That Lady Edith is so full of herself," Freya said. "She's all '*Ooh, Angle Land is sooo great, what?*'. She's driving me mad!"

"You think you've got problems?" said Knut, who stood on Vulgar's right. His cheeks were red and swollen from being pinched. "I look like I'm carrying nuts home for the winter."

"Well, let's do something about it then," Vulgar said. "We'll teach these Anglish a lesson."

"Maybe we should've brought Dagmar the Dull after all," Knut said.

"Not *that* sort of lesson," Vulgar said. "A proper *Viking* lesson. We'll show them how tough we really are – and take home their gold as a souvenir."

As Vulgar whispered his plan, Lady Edith and King Olaf stepped out on to the battlefield.

"Attention, everyone!" boomed Lady Edith, her voice carrying like cannon fire across the battlefield. "Today marks the one hundredth anniversary of the Battle of Burp where, as you all know, the good people of Burp gave the Vikings of Blubber a proper thrashing."

"Well, I don't know about that—" said King Olaf.

"A real hammering," Edith continued. "Bash, biff, pow, take that, you helmet-wearing chumps!"

King Olaf smiled weakly. "Steady on."

"We will re-enact that glorious event this very day. Upon my command we shall commence battle, whereupon the villagers of Burp shall thrash the living daylights out of the Vikings of Blubber, exactly as we did a century ago."

"We were having a bad day, that's all," King Olaf protested.

"I'll say," snorted Lady Edith. "Your chaps ended up swimming home in their underpants."

"Can we get on with it?" asked Vulgar.

Lady Edith and King Olaf glared at each other for a moment, then turned and smiled brightly at the assembled children.

"Have fun," said King Olaf. "And may the better side win."

"Oh, don't worry, we already did," said Lady Edith, then she and King Olaf marched off the battlefield, leaving the children of Burp and Blubber to face off.

Each side stood behind their shields, eyeballing one another across the battlefield.

"Come for our gold, have you?" cried a voice from the Burp side. "You'll have to get through us first."

"My granny could get through you lot," shouted someone from Vulgar's class.

"It's a pity you didn't bring her, then," replied a boy from Burp. "You lot need all the help you can get."

The Burp side erupted in laughter.

That did it. Vulgar raised his sword. He gritted his teeth. "Vikings," he commanded. *"Chaaaaaarge!"*

Both sides ran towards the centre of the field, swords waggling, shields waving. They clattered together in the middle, swishing and swiping as weapons clashed against kitchen utensils.

Albert swung a frying pan at Vulgar, but Vulgar was ready for him. He deflected the blow with his shield and thrust with his sword. Albert dodged out of the way and both boys began to circle one another.

Knut, meanwhile, was spread out on the ground. "Ack, I've been killed," he said. He closed his eyes. "May as well have a nap while I'm down here."

Freya was locking swords with Gilbert, who was armed with a rolling pin. She suddenly dropped her sword and clutched at her stomach. "Argh," she yelped. "You have bested me in battle!"

Gilbert looked surprised. "Have I?"

"Yes. You have," confirmed Freya, then she flopped on to the ground and

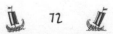

played dead.

Gilbert gave a huge grin and put his hands on his hips. "Ha!" he said. "Of course I could beat a silly *girl*."

Freya opened one eye and Gilbert quickly jumped backwards. "Don't push it," she growled, then she went back to being dead.

Albert drew back his frying pan, but Vulgar fell over before he could swing.

"Oh dear," he said. "I am beaten. Boo-hoo." Vulgar bit his lip and tried not to laugh. It was his turn to play a trick on the twins. One that they wouldn't forget in a hurry!

With a cheer, the twins raced off to join the rest of the Burp children. They were forcing their way through the Blubber army using the Boar's Snout technique. Soon it would all be over and Burp would be victorious. Again.

Or so they thought. When the battle had moved on, Vulgar opened his eyes. He gave Knut a shake.

"Not the cheeks again!" Knut spluttered, waking with a start. Vulgar had to put a hand over his mouth to silence him.

"Come on," Vulgar whispered to Freya.

"We don't have much time."

Vulgar, Knut and Freya crawled away from the fighting, trying not to get attacked.

A boy from Blubber charged at a boy from Burp, who was wearing a colander as a helmet and holding a saucepan lid as a shield. The Blubber boy knocked the lid out of the Burp child's hand and shouted, "Put that in your pot and cook it!"

Nearby, a girl from Burp whacked a girl from Blubber on the head with a baking tray. "How'd you like the taste of *that*!" she cried as the Blubber girl fell to the grass, defeated.

As the battle raged, Vulgar, Knut and Freya hurried up the hill. When they got to the tower, Vulgar looked back at the battlefield. Some of the Viking children seemed to have forgotten that they were supposed to lose the battle. They were putting up a brave fight, but more of them were lying defeated on the ground than the Burp children. There was no time to lose.

"Quick! Head to the top!" Vulgar ordered Knut and Freya. He locked the heavy door behind them, then pounded up the stairs.

From the window at the top of the tower, they watched as a beaming Lady Edith stepped out into the field. A great cheer rose from the children of Burp.

"A rousing, well-deserved victory," she announced, applauding wildly. "The battle is over and, just as was the case one hundred years ago, the fine upstanding people of Burp have driven back the wretched, pilfering, smelly Vikings!"

"Not this time, you haven't!" Vulgar shouted from the window, grinning at the people below. "When you weren't looking,

we conquered the tower.
And now we're going to
loot your gold. Don't
think you can stop us,
because we've locked the
door." He held up the
key, laughing.

Lady Edith's face darkened. "Throw me
that key at once," she commanded.

"You want it?" called Vulgar. He pulled
back his arm. "Go get it!"

He tossed the key as hard as he could. It
sailed through the air, over the cliffs, and
then plunged into the sea far below.

"Now you'll never get in," said
Vulgar in triumph.

"But we'll never get *out*, you idiot,"
Freya hissed.

Vulgar's face fell. "Oh yeah," he said.
"I didn't think of that."

CHAPTER SIX

TRAPPED IN THE TOWER

Vulgar paced around the tiny room. Freya glared at him, her toe tapping impatiently. In the corner, Knut was having a nap.

"OK, let me think about this," Vulgar said. "We've locked the door. We've thrown away the key."

"*You've* thrown away the key," Freya snapped.

"That's not helping!" Vulgar told her.

"At least we've got the
Burp gold."

Freya looked around
the room. "What gold?"

Vulgar stopped pacing. "It's... um... It
must be in another room."

"There *are* no other rooms, Vulgar,"
Freya said. "It's just this and lots of stairs!"

Vulgar tutted. "Great. So we're locked
in the tower with no key and no gold
either. This is turning into a disaster."

"*Turning into* a disaster?" Freya

spluttered. "It's a full-blown disaster with a catastrophe on top. You got us into this mess, so you can get us out of it."

"But—"

Freya pointed to the window. "Get us out of here, Vulgar. Now."

Vulgar dragged his feet over to the window. He leaned out. "Yoo hoo!" he called out, smiling nervously. "All that stuff I said a minute ago, about us stealing your gold. You know I was joking, right?"

The crowd glared up at him. He cleared his throat. "Anyway, we were wondering. Does anyone have a ladder?"

Lady Edith leaped into action. "You two, run to the village and fetch a ladder," she barked, pointing to two of the Burp children.

"You two, go and help them," King Olaf commanded, choosing two of the

Blubber children.

When the children returned with the ladder, King Olaf and Lady Edith heaved it into position at the base of the tower. Vulgar and Freya peered down.

"It's a bit short, isn't it?" said Vulgar. The ladder stopped several metres below the window ledge.

"Could you jump, do you think?" called King Olaf.

"Not if we want to live," Vulgar replied. He thought about this. "Hey Freya, why don't you try?"

Freya elbowed him in the ribs. "It's no use," she shouted to her father. "Try breaking down the door."

"Right you are, petal," replied King Olaf. "We'll have you out of there in two shakes of a reindeer's tail."

King Olaf studied the heavy wood. He rapped his knuckles against it. "This is going to hurt," he announced. He took a deep breath and stepped backwards. "Harrumf," he said. "Break it down."

Harrumf looked round in surprise. "What? Me?"

"Well you can't expect me to do it," said the King. "I'm royalty."

"What about her, then?" Vulgar called down, pointing at Lady Edith. "She's built like a carthorse."

"I beg your pardon!" Lady Edith gasped.

Muttering, Harrumf took a few shaky

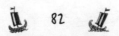

steps away from the door. "Right then.
'Ave some of this." With a roar he
charged towards the door, slamming his
shoulder against the wood.

There was a *thud*.

There was a yelp.

"Ouch. That looked painful," Vulgar
whispered to Freya.

Harrumf bounced backwards and
landed face down on the wet grass.

King Olaf shook his head in dismay.
"You weren't even trying," he said. "Use
the other shoulder."

"It's no use," sighed Lady Edith. "That
door could withstand a charging bull."

"Well what are we supposed to do?
Leave them in there?"

"Leave us?" Freya cried. "They're going
to leave us! We're going to be stuck in here
forever!"

"Still, it could be worse," said Vulgar.

"How?" snapped Freya.

Vulgar thought about it. "No, you're right. It couldn't be worse."

Gazing out of the window, Vulgar saw Albert and Gilbert pointing up at him and waving. But then they smiled and ran off down the hill together. "Oh no," Vulgar groaned. "Not another one of their pranks." It looked like things *could* get worse – if the Terrible Twosome started throwing tomatoes at the tower or launching jellyfish through the window.

But moments later, he saw the boys heading back up the hill, dragging something behind them. Vulgar couldn't see what it was, but even from way up in the tower he recognised the fishy smell.

Vulgar cheered. "They've brought a net!"

Albert and Gilbert waved up at him as the crowd gathered around the wide net.

They stretched it out, pulling it tight above the ground.

"Jump," urged King Olaf. "We'll catch you."

"You go first," Vulgar said, nudging Freya towards the window.

"No! You go first."

"You're a princess."

"So you should check that it's safe."

"I'm starving. I'll go first," said Knut, who was suddenly wide awake. He walked over to the window, put a hand on top of his helmet, and jumped.

With a *boing*, Knut landed safely in the net.

"*Now* I'll go," Freya said. She swung her legs over the ledge, closed her eyes, and jumped. Vulgar watched her bounce in the net, then scramble down on to solid ground.

Vulgar swallowed hard. The net looked a long way away. He wanted to jump, but his feet were frozen in place. He couldn't do it. He was too sca—

"Come on," shouted Gilbert. "You're Vulgar the Viking!"

"You're the bravest warrior in the world!" Albert cheered.

Vulgar puffed out his chest. The boys were right. He was Vulgar the Viking, and Vikings weren't afraid of anything.

He stood on the window ledge. He held out his arms.

And then he jumped out as far as he could go. Only it was a bit too far. Vulgar was headed straight for the flag pole! He

reached out and
grabbed it. Vulgar swung
around it like a gymnast – once,
twice, three times. *WHOOSH!*
WHOOSH! WHOOSH!

Then he lost his grip...

"AAAAARRRRGGGHHHHH!" he
shrieked as he plummeted towards the
ground.

BOING!

Vulgar bounced into
the net, somersaulted
once, and landed
perfectly on his feet.

The crowd cheered, and suddenly two sets of arms were wrapped around him, hugging him tightly. He looked down into the twins' freckled faces.

"That was *amazing*!" Gilbert said.

"When I'm bigger, I want to be a proper Viking," said Albert. "Just like you!"

"Oh, it was nothing," Vulgar said happily.

"You children have been very silly, what?" Lady Edith scolded. "Capture the Burp gold indeed. There *is* no Burp gold. It was used up long ago to build the statue you saw. Nowadays our only treasure is cheese."

"And fish," said Bert. He and Bertha were making their way up the hill carrying a huge iron pot.

"Fried fish and potatoes," Bertha said. "We thought you might be hungry after the battle."

"Now you're talking," Knut said with a grin.

"I think a picnic is in order," Lady Edith announced.

King Olaf looked up at the grey sky. "What, in this rain?"

"Of course," snorted Lady Edith, clapping the King on the back. "Didn't you know? It's *always* raining in Angle Land!"

Chattering and laughing, the children sat on the wet grass and tucked into the food. Even Vulgar had to admit it tasted great. The fish had been covered in some sort of breadcrumb coating, and the potatoes had been cut into little stick shapes.

"How do you make these?" he asked, peering at one of the potato sticks.

"Oh, it's not difficult," said Bertha. "We just sort of chip away at them."

Albert and Gilbert appeared beside him. Vulgar covered his head when he realised they were both holding tomatoes.

But the twins squidged the tomatoes into a runny paste on Vulgar's plate. "Dip the sticks in that," they said. "It tastes great!"

Vulgar did as they suggested, and they were right. It did taste great.

"Thanks for helping me out," Vulgar said to the twins.

"S'OK," explained Gilbert, through a mouthful of fish and chips. "We'd never let our big brother down!"

"Except if he needed to get down," added Albert.

Vulgar smiled. Big brother. He liked the sound of that.

After the picnic they played a sport that involved kicking an inflated bladder around the field. Vulgar scored three goals, although the game had to be abandoned when Knut tried to header the bladder and it burst on the one horn that stuck up from his helmet.

Then it was time for the Blubber children to head back to the longboat. They said their goodbyes and hugged their host families. Knut even allowed the old woman to give him one last pinch on the cheek. Albert and Gilbert gave Vulgar a bag with a pig's bladder and a large starfish in it. Vulgar couldn't wait to try out the new pranks on the unsuspecting people of Blubber. Who needed gold when you had a starfish to stick in your parents' bed?!

Vulgar had gone to Burp in search of battle, but he'd found allies instead.

As they stood on the dock waving him goodbye, Vulgar called out to the twins, "I'll come back one day! And we'll go pillaging together!"

And with the sound of King Olaf's singing ringing loudly in his ears, Vulgar heaved the oars and began the long row home.